RUSS T

NEVER
WANTED

Bookstock Press

Editing by Laura Perkins. Series concept by Pam Sheppard. Cover by Shayne at Wicked Good Book Covers. Print text set in Open Dyslexic Mono. File HP003.27D.2021.06.04. Website www.bookstockpress.com.

Lexile measure HL530L.

For Betty-Jean,
our kids,
and grandkids.

CONTENTS

1 TEN

WEDNESDAY MORNING. ENGLISH. Ms. Gulliver tells us we have to work harder.

Boring.

She turns and writes on the whiteboard. I pick up my English book and throw it out the window.

Henry looks down and smiles. Someone behind me laughs.

Ms. Gulliver turns around. Her face is red, and she's mad.

"You're not little kids," she says. "This is the tenth grade.

Whoever is doing it, quit playing around."

It felt good to see that book go flying out the window.

CLASS ENDS. Henry and I walk down the hall.

"Roy, why did you throw that book?" he asks.

"I don't know. It just happened."

"But it had your desk number on it."

The principal, Dr. Vinson, walks by. He carries the book I threw.

I think I'm caught.

HISTORY. Mr. Rubio comes to the front of the classroom.

"Clear your desks," he says. "When you get your test, keep it face down until I say turn it over."

I don't know the answer to the first question, so I guess C. On the next one, I guess D.

I used to care about my grades. I don't know when I stopped.

The door opens. It's Dr. Vinson. "Roy, come with me," he says.

I follow him into the empty hallway. I know what's coming.

"Why did you throw that book out the window?" he asks.

"What book?"

"The one you threw out of Ms. Gulliver's class."

"It wasn't me."

"Why did it have your desk number on it?"

"I don't know."

He pulls out a detention slip, fills it out, and gives me the pink copy.

It's no big deal. I've had detention plenty of times.

But he pulls out his phone.

"Wait," I say. "You don't have to call. I'll do double detention."

"You've already had that," he says. "But you keep messing up."

"Please don't. I'm begging you."

He looks at me and makes the call.

"Hello, Mr. Newberry?... This is Dr. Vinson from Edison High School. Roy has been given detention again... He threw a book out the window of his English class... I know you will... Thanks for speaking with me."

Dr. Vinson probably thinks he's smart.

He doesn't know what Uncle Frank is going to do to me.

FIVE O'CLOCK. Uncle Frank's truck pulls up outside our trailer.

I know he'll be drunk. But I hope he's not real drunk. The more he drinks, the meaner he gets.

The wooden steps creak. The front door bangs open.

He comes inside and glares at me. He smells like beer, lots of beer.

I can feel what's going to happen to me.

"You know what to do," he says.

I try not to shake. I pull out my chair from the kitchen table, turn it around, and put my hands on the seat.

I try to keep my voice calm. "How many?"

He takes off his belt and folds it in half. "I don't know yet."

I bend over, put my hands on the

seat, and brace myself.

Whack!

The pain shoots through me.

Whack!

The stinging goes down the back of my legs.

Whack!

He's hitting me as hard as he can.

I close my eyes. I can't take any more.

He reaches ten.

"Get up," he says.

I limp to my room, close the door, and fall face down on my bed.

I hate him.

2 GRADES

THURSDAY MORNING. Seven o-clock. I walk into the kitchen.

Uncle Frank is already gone. I'm glad I don't have to look at him.

I pick up his empty beer bottles and throw them in the trash can. I can still feel him hitting me.

It was worse when Mom was alive.

We had a trailer out in the desert. Her boyfriend would slap me and call me trash.

All the fighting. All the drugs. They would lock me in my bedroom and cook meth in the kitchen.

I was only ten.

TIME TO LEAVE. School starts in thirty minutes.

Henry's trailer is five spaces down. I knock on his door. We put down our skateboards and go.

He jumps the first curb like it's nothing.

My glute muscles still hurt from last night. I can barely skate, so I don't even try.

We turn left at Jupiter Street.

"How many times did he hit you?" Henry asks.

"I don't want to talk about it."

LUNCH. The detention room is crowded. I finish my sandwich. It feels better to sit down now.

The lady in charge brings me a blank detention sheet.

I write as fast as I can. It doesn't have to be good. I just have to make it sound like I'm sorry.

Name: Roy Perkins
Detention given by: Dr. Vinson

My Goals

I want to get better in school. I can do it by working harder.

I know I shouldn't have thrown that book out the window of Ms. Gulliver's class.

Dr. Vinson caught me. Now I'm paying for it.

Ms. Gulliver is a nice lady. I'm sorry for what I did.

I don't know why I did it. It

just happened.

School books cost a lot of money. When I threw it out the window, it landed in mud.

That made it worse. Now I'm in here for three days.

My Uncle Frank works construction. He's on a job now in Gilmore.

It's an hour drive to get there. He always gets home late.

His truck is falling apart. Sometimes it doesn't start. The brakes are also bad.

I've been living with him for five years.

I'm supposed to write about how I will improve in school. My grades aren't good right now.

I know I can get better. I know I have to quit playing around. But *sometimes, things happen.*

I want to have a good life and be somebody.

AFTERNOON. Home from school. It's nice to be here by myself.

I sit at the kitchen table and open the laptop. It's an old one with a busted hinge. I had to fix it with duct tape.

I get on School View and go to the section for grades.

I don't want to look. But maybe they will be okay.

I have a B in PE. But I have NoPasses in English, Spanish, history, science, and math.

These are the worst grades I've ever had.

3 JUST SKATE

FRIDAY MORNING. ENGLISH. Ms. Gulliver smiles when I come in the door.

I don't know why she's so nice to me after I threw her book out the window.

I could never be that way.

We're writing essays about the reading she gave us. She kneels next to my desk.

"I read your detention paper," she says. "Nice job."

"Thanks."

"I also looked at your grades in School View. I know you can bring them up. You just have to start doing the work."

She's wrong about my grades. They will never come up.

She has no idea what I'm going through.

HISTORY. Mr. Rubio hands back the test papers from yesterday. Mine is another NoPass.

Every day gets worse.

He comes to the front of the classroom.

"Today, we start on World War One," he says. "Read page 206. I will then call on you to answer some questions."

I try to read. But it's hard to concentrate.

My clothes probably smell. We ran out of laundry soap last week.

I remember how it was in the third grade. My clothes were always dirty.

A kid named Jimmy told me I smelled bad. I socked him for saying it.

Mom came with me the next morning to see the principal.

She was wearing her nice clothes.

I still had on my dirty clothes from the day before.

All I wanted was clean clothes so the kids wouldn't laugh at me.

"Time's up," Mr. Rubio says. "Which countries fought during World War One?"

I keep my hand down. I don't want him to call on me.

"Roy, could you answer?" he asks.

"I don't know."

"When did the war start?"

"I don't know."

"When did the war end?"

Someone calls out from the back.
"He doesn't know."

AFTER SCHOOL. I meet Henry by the
math building.

We unlock our skateboards and go
out the front gate.

"Red Church?" he asks.

"Sure."

My legs feel better now. We skate
for ten minutes and turn left into
the alley.

The Red Church has a big concrete
space next to the parking lot. It
doesn't have any cracks, so it's
great for skating.

We do ground tricks, mostly kickflips and ollies.

The nice thing about skating, is that I don't have to think about anything.

I need new wheels. But other than that, everything is great.

No problems. Just skate.

4 ALL ALONE

FRIDAY AFTERNOON. I climb the wooden steps and open the front door to our trailer.

Uncle Frank isn't home yet.

Good.

I'm still mad about what happened in history. I get on the laptop, go to YouTube, and type in World War One into the search box.

The first video shows a submarine sinking a ship. Smoke pours out of it. Then the ship goes under.

The next video shows soldiers

charging across a field with bombs going off. Many of the soldiers fall.

It's exciting to watch the videos at first. Then I realize they show real people getting killed.

That's how my dad died, when a bomb blew up under his army truck.

Things were never the same after that.

Mom fell apart.

She started using drugs.

Everything went bad.

SIX O'CLOCK. Uncle Frank still isn't home yet. I guess he's drinking extra late.

I turn on the TV and pull a blanket over me.

When I first came to live with Uncle Frank, he was nice.

We built a bike together out of old parts. He showed me how to fix things. If I did something wrong, he would talk to me, not hit me.

Then he went back to drinking.

He would slap me on the side of the head and tell me I was nothing.

TWO HOURS LATER. A car pulls up outside. I look out the window.

It's a police car.

Two officers walk up the steps and knock on the door.

"Roy Perkins?" the older cop asks.

I let them inside. Something is wrong.

"It's about your uncle," the younger cop says. "He was driving under the influence and hit a lady crossing the street. She died."

I look at him, but I'm not sure what to say. Uncle Frank beats me. But he's the only family I have.

"What's going to happen to me?" I ask.

"Your uncle is being held at County Jail," the older cop says. "A social worker will take you to a place to stay tonight."

"Where will that be?"

"It could be with a family. Or you might go to a group home."

I feel like I'm falling.

I'm all alone.

5 NOT SURE

LATER. I sit in the living room with the two cops.

A car pulls up outside. Someone comes up the steps.

She's old, probably about forty, with a worn-out look on her face.

"Roy, I'm Ms. Fenster from Family Services," she says. "We have a place for you to stay."

"Where?"

"It's with a family. They live close to here."

This is it. I'm leaving.

I go to my room, open my duffel bag, and stuff in my clothes. All of them are dirty.

I grab my backpack and skateboard. I also grab the laptop.

One more thing.

I go into Uncle Frank's room, pull up the heating vent, and reach inside.

The first sock has a wad of money, three-hundred bucks.

The second sock has the box of bullets.

The third sock has the gun, a nine-millimeter.

I put it all in my duffel bag.

The gun worries me. But it doesn't feel right to leave it.

TIME TO LEAVE. We go outside. The cops lock the trailer.

I get in the car with Ms. Fenster. She pulls away. I wonder if I'll ever be back.

"The people you're going to stay with are the Radleys," she says. "I think you'll like them."

I look out the side window and pretend not to hear her.

"Was your uncle drinking a lot?" she asks.

"Nothing bad," I say. "Just sometimes."

"What about food? The refrigerator was almost empty."

"This was our night to get burgers."

"What about school? How has that been going?"

"Fine."

I don't know why I lie to her. It seems like the thing to do.

She turns right onto Orchard
Avenue.

The yards look nice. The houses
look nice.

It's another world.

MS. FENSTER PARKS. We're at a yellow
house with a big tree and flowers.

I follow her to the front door.
It opens before she knocks.

The lady smiles like she's glad
to see me. The man smiles, too.

"This is Mr. and Ms. Radley," Ms.
Fenster says.

Ms. Radley is pretty. She reminds
me of Mom before things went bad.
"We're glad to have you with us,"
she says.

Mr. Radley is big, like he used
to play football. "We're sorry about
what happened. We're going to make

this as good as we can for you."

They seem like nice people. I hope it's true.

I step inside and put my stuff down.

It's like a perfect house from a TV show. I've never lived in a nice place before.

"Let's go into the kitchen," Ms. Radley says. "I bet you're hungry."

I sit at the table. She brings me a warm plate of food. It's chicken, with rice and vegetables on the side.

I haven't had a regular meal in a long time.

"When was the last time you ate?" Ms. Radley asks.

"Lunch. I had a ham sandwich."

It was really chips and doughnuts. I don't know why I lie.

"How long will I be staying here?" I ask.

"We don't know," Mr. Radley says. "It depends on what happens with your uncle."

I begin eating. The food is good. The house is nice. And the Radleys are nice.

But I don't feel at home.

ELEVEN O'CLOCK. Ms. Radley takes me into the spare bedroom. Folded pajamas lie on top of the bed.

"When you're ready to take a shower, I put some fresh towels in the bathroom," she says. "We know you're going through a lot. Things are going to be okay."

She closes the door. I look around the room. It's plain, but nice. Maybe it will be okay.

I hide the money and gun under the mattress. It's not the greatest hiding place. But it's the best I can do.

I go down the hall to the bathroom. It seems strange to take a hot shower. All we had in the trailer was cold water.

I walk back to my room. The duffel bag is empty.

What's going on?

I go to the kitchen. Ms. Radley is cleaning up.

I try not to sound mad. "Where are my clothes?"

"They're in the washer," she says. "They'll be dry and ready for you in the morning."

I don't like the idea that she went through my stuff. I'm glad I hid the gun.

Mr. Radley comes in. "Tomorrow, you get to meet the twins," he says. "They're five years old, Marcus and Milo. They'll be knocking on your door in the morning. They're foster kids."

I go back to my room and get under the covers.

It's nice to have clean sheets. And nobody is going to hit me.

But I'm not sure about Ms. Radley.

6 DOESN'T KNOW

SATURDAY MORNING. I hear footsteps run down the hall. My bedroom door bangs open.

"I'm Marcus," the first one says. He's wearing pajamas with fire trucks.

"I'm Milo," the second one says. He's wearing pajamas with bulldozers and dump trucks.

"Mom told us you were nice," Marcus says. "Are you going to be our brother?"

"I don't know."

"We're twins," Milo says. "We go to Longfellow School."

"What grade?"

"We're in kindergarten," Marcus says. "We have Ms. Butterfield."

They run out and slam the door.

I hope I get to stay here.

BREAKFAST. I go into the kitchen. Mr. Radley comes in.

He has a badge and gun on his belt. I try not to stare, but he sees me.

"I didn't tell you last night because a lot was happening," he says. "I'm a detective with the Conroy Police Department."

The badge and gun make me nervous. I don't like that he's a cop.

"How late do you think you'll be

tonight?" Ms. Radley asks him.

"Not sure," Mr. Radley says. "The team worked all last night. It depends on what they found."

"What about the owner?" Ms. Radley asks.

"He made it out of surgery," Mr. Radley says. "But he's still in bad shape."

I wish I didn't have Uncle Frank's gun.

I should have left it in the trailer.

PRICE MART. The parking lot is crowded. Ms. Radley finds a spot near the back.

"Marcus and Milo, you hold hands with Roy," Ms. Radley says. "I don't want you getting hit by any of these cars."

I hold their hands as we walk through the parking lot. They squeeze tight. It makes me feel like a big brother.

Ms. Radley gets me three pairs of blue uniform pants and three uniform shirts.

I look at the price tags. They cost a lot of money.

Next, we go to sporting goods.

"I noticed you didn't have a skateboard helmet," Ms. Radley says.

I don't want a helmet. But I don't have a choice. I pick a black one that costs twenty-two dollars.

What I really need are skateboard wheels. But with the helmet and school clothes, that would be too much money.

"Groceries are next," Ms. Radley says.

"Is it okay if I look around for a while?" I ask.

"Sure," Ms. Radley says. "Come find us when you're done."

I go back to the skateboard section. The wheels I need cost twenty-nine dollars.

I don't want to take them. But I don't feel right about asking Ms. Radley to spend more money on me.

Nobody is watching. I slip the wheels into the hole I cut in the lining of my jacket.

I feel the weight of them. But I know they don't show from the outside.

GROCERY SECTION. I find Ms. Radley and the twins. The cart is full of food.

"Time to pay for this stuff and

go home," Ms. Radley says.

Marcus and Milo hold my hands as we walk to the front.

I wish I hadn't taken the wheels. But it's too late to put them back.

I look away from the cashier as we go through the checkout line. I keep an eye out for security on the way to the van.

I'm glad when we make it out of the parking lot.

AFTERNOON. Ms. Radley said I could skate for an hour. I meet Henry at the Red Church.

"What's with the helmet?" Henry asks.

I take it off and put it on the ground. "Ms. Radley got it for me."

"How much did the wheels cost?"

"Nothing."

Henry shakes his head. "You're being stupid again. What if you had been caught?"

"Don't worry about it."

We begin skating.

Henry is my friend. But he doesn't know what I'm going through.

7 IF I CAN

MONDAY MORNING. I say goodbye to Ms. Radley and leave for school.

I don't like wearing my helmet, but I have to. I put down my skateboard and go.

The corner at the end of Orchard Avenue has bushes by the sidewalk. I hide the helmet under them and keep skating.

Ms. Radley will never know.

LUNCH. I walk by the drinking fountain. Somebody pushes my

shoulder.

It's Donny.

He's on the basketball team, one of the biggest guys in the school.

"Your uncle killed that lady," Donny says. "I'm glad he's in jail."

I know I'm going to get in trouble. But I don't care.

I swing up and punch him in the jaw.

He comes back at me and swings with his right.

I duck and sock him in the ribs.

He swings again.

I nail him in the stomach.

Somebody grabs me from behind and lifts me off my feet.

PRINCIPAL'S OFFICE. I sit across the desk from Dr. Vinson. His shirt is wrinkled from breaking up the fight.

"Roy, why did you hit him?" he asks.

"Donny always has something to say."

"Like what?"

"Talking about my uncle. He needs to shut up."

"Is that what you do? You hit people if they say something wrong to you?"

"Sometimes."

Dr. Vinson calls Mr. Radley. I don't want to be in trouble. But I did what I did.

And it was fun seeing the look on Donny's face when I punched him in the jaw.

LATER. I'm suspended for the rest of the day. I ride in the front seat with Mr. Radley in his detective car.

It surprises me when he pulls
into Burger House. We order and sit
at a table by the window.

"What was the fight about?" Mr.
Radley asks.

"He talked about my uncle."

"Did you have to hit him?"

"No. But I wanted to."

They call our number. We get our
food from the front counter.

"What if he has medical bills?"
Mr. Radley asks. "Who's going to pay
them?"

"I don't know."

"We want you to stay with us," he
says. "But you have to think. You
also have to be a good role model
for Marcus and Milo."

"Like how?"

"You have to set a positive

example."

I take a bite of my hamburger. I think about all the times when I've been hungry.

"Life is what you make of it," Mr. Radley says. "It's about the decisions you make. Every time you make a good decision, it helps you. Every time you make a bad one, it holds you back."

I know he's right. I know I have to change.

But I don't know if I can.

8 BIGGER THAN ME

TUESDAY MORNING. It's almost time
for the bell to ring.

I run through the gate and to the
guidance room. It's my first day of
in-school suspension.

The guidance room is like a
regular classroom, but with the
desks spread apart.

Donny sits away from me. He tries
to hide his face. But I can see the
swelling and bruising where I hit
him in the jaw.

I may be skinny. But I can fight.

That's one thing I learned from Uncle Frank.

The lady in charge gives us our work. The first assignment is to write an essay about why I'm here.

I begin writing.

Roy Perkins
In-School Suspension

Why I'm Here

I try not to get in trouble. But sometimes things just happen. And you can't do much about it when certain things go wrong.

It made me mad when Donny talked about my uncle. He had no right to do that.

He thinks he can push people around because he's bigger than they are.

Some people don't have a nice life, like others do. They don't have nice things and a nice home to go to.

Not everybody has a good family. Sometimes the parents have problems. They do bad things that hurt their kids. But it's not the fault of the kids.

I'm living in a new place now. Maybe it will be better for me.

TEN-THIRTY. Mr. Wiley, the dean, comes into the guidance room.

He motions for Donny and me to follow him into his office.

"We're here to get this straight," Mr. Wiley says. "I don't want any more problems between you two. I'm going to read your essays.

Then we're going to have a mediation."

We wait while he reads our papers. I think about what I wrote.

"Both of you were wrong," Mr. Wiley says. "Donny, you should have kept your mouth shut. Roy, you should have walked away."

It's easy for him to say that. He doesn't know what it feels like when your life is hard.

We take turns talking and shake hands.

I know Donny doesn't mean it when he says he's sorry.

I don't mean it either. He started it. And I finished it.

I would do it again if I had to.

LUNCH. Donny and I sit in the guidance room.

I wish I could go outside. But staying here for lunch is part of the punishment.

I open my backpack and eat the turkey sandwich I made. It has cheese, lettuce, and tomato.

The Radleys have good food. It's not the donuts and chips I would buy at Mike's Market when I was living with Uncle Frank.

Donny eats his lunch too. I can tell he's still mad.

TWO O'CLOCK. Mr. Wiley brings us back into his office.

We have to sign a contract that we won't fight again. We also have to explain what we should have done.

I'm not going to start anything. But I'm pretty sure Donny will come after me again.

I made him look bad because I won
the fight and he's bigger than me.

9 MESSED UP

SCHOOL'S OUT. I walk to the exit.
It's nice to be out of the guidance
room.

Henry stands by the skateboard
racks. "You ready?"

"Yep."

We unlock our boards and go out
the front gate.

The crowd outside is bigger than
normal.

"Looks like there's going to be a
fight," Henry says.

Someone shoves me from behind.

I turn around.

It's Donny.

He stares at me with his fists balled up.

I stare back at him, right into his eyes.

If he swings, I'm going to nail him.

A big guy from the basketball team steps between us. He pushes Donny away from me.

"What's wrong with you?" he says to Donny. "Coach Reed will have us running forever if you fight again."

They turn away and walk toward the gym.

"Hurry up," Henry says. "Let's get out of here."

NEPTUNE STREET. Henry and I stop at a red light.

"Are you okay?" he asks.

"I'm okay now. But I know that Donny is going to come after me again."

"What are you going to do?"

"I don't know."

RADLEY'S HOUSE. I open the front door. It feels good to step inside.

But something is wrong. Ms. Radley sits in the living room. She's been waiting for me.

She follows me into my bedroom with a bag in her hand.

"We need to talk," she says. "I found something this morning."

She opens the bag and pulls out the package from the skateboard wheels I stole.

"It was in the trash can," she says.

I have to think quickly. But I don't know what to say.

She picks up my skateboard and spins the wheels. "When did you get these? They seem new."

"Uncle Frank got them for me. My other wheels were getting flat spots."

"Did you know that I used to be a cop?" Ms. Radley says. "We had a lot of training. One of the things they taught us, was how to spot a liar."

She knows what I did. How will I get out of this?

"When you told me about the wheels, your eyes darted up and to the left. You also covered your mouth with your hand."

"But I'm telling the truth."

"You did it again," she says. "I'll let you think about it."

She leaves the room and closes
the door.

I messed up.

10 BROTHER

KITCHEN. I sit at the table with Marcus and Milo. They're doing worksheets for their kindergarten class.

Ms. Radley says I have to do my homework with them to be a role model.

I start English first. We have to read for twenty minutes in a book of our choice and write a paragraph on how we feel about it.

I finish reading and write my paragraph. Marcus and Milo finish their worksheets and begin drawing pictures. It's fun to watch them.

Next, I start on history. We have to read and answer questions. After that, I have science to do.

I never used to do my homework so soon after school. I would wait until the last minute and do a rush job.

Sometimes, I wouldn't do it at all.

I'm trying to go the right way now.

SIX O'CLOCK. We sit at the kitchen table for dinner.

"Where's Dad?" Marcus asks.

"He's still on the robbery case from Saturday," Ms. Radley says. "He's staying on it because the store owner was hurt so bad."

I think about the gun under my bed. I wish I didn't have it.

"Does he have to work late all the time?" I ask.

Ms. Radley puts her napkin in her lap. "He's chief of detectives, so he has to go out on all the big cases. Sometimes he has to work twenty-four hours straight."

I didn't know he was a chief. I thought he was just a regular detective.

We begin eating. The front door opens. Mr. Radley walks in.

"We made the arrest this afternoon," he says.

He takes off his jacket and sits down with us.

I see the badge and gun on his belt. I wonder if I could be a cop someday.

"Roy, how was in-school suspension?" he asks.

"We had to sit there and do work the whole time. We also had to stay in there for lunch."

"Did you learn anything?"

"Mr. Wiley said I wasn't thinking when I hit the other guy. He told me not to let my emotions control me."

"That's a good lesson."

I carry my plate to the kitchen sink and rinse it. "I'll be glad when it's over. It's like being in jail."

"Sounds like it's making you think," Mr. Radley says. "That's good."

I have to get rid of the gun.

AFTER DINNER. I sit on the living-room floor with Marcus and Milo.

We're building things with their Legos.

Marcus builds a car. Milo makes a spaceship.

During all my time as a kid, I never had anybody watch over me. I was always by myself.

I made things with Legos in my room while my mom and her boyfriend cooked meth.

I hope I get to stay. I would like to be a brother to Marcus and Milo.

11   STILL SHAKES

NINE O'CLOCK. I sit in my room. I can't stop thinking about what Mr. Radley said. I want to show him I'm responsible.

I lift the mattress and pull out the gun.

Mr. Radley will be proud of me for giving it to him. But I have to unload it first.

I push a button on the handle. The clip with the bullets drops out.

The gun is safe now.

I wonder what it feels like to

pull the trigger.

I point the gun at the floor.

Boom!

Smoke comes out the barrel.
There's a hole in the wooden floor
by my shoe.

What have I done?

Mr. Radley bursts into the room.
He steps behind me and takes the gun
from my hand.

Ms. Radley also runs in.

Tears go down my face.

"Roy, it's okay," Mr. Radley
says. "Nobody got hurt. You took the
clip out. But there was still a
bullet in the chamber."

Marcus and Milo come in. Their
bedroom is next door. I could have
shot one of them.

My hand still shakes.

12 WHY DID I?

LIVING ROOM. I sit on the couch with Mr. and Mrs. Radley.

Ms. Radley puts her arm around me. I was wrong about her before. I can tell she really cares.

The police get here, two of them. They go into my bedroom and come out with the gun in a plastic bag.

The older cop sits across from me. I try not to shake.

"Where did you get the gun?" he asks.

"It was my uncle's. I brought it

when I came to live here."

"Why did you do that?"

"I don't know. I just did it."

"Why did your uncle have it?"

"I don't know. I found it in his room one day when I was looking around."

They speak with Mr. Radley in the kitchen. I can't hear what they say.

They're probably going to come in and put handcuffs on me.

The officers come back with Mr. Radley. "You did a stupid thing," the older officer says. "Make sure you learn from it."

They leave and drive away. I thought for sure I was going to be arrested.

Mr. Radley sits down next to me.

"You're lucky you didn't blow your foot off," he says. "And if you had shot through the wall, you could have hit one of the twins."

"I'm sorry."

"I know you're sorry," Mr. Radley says. "And I know you'll never do it again. But this is bad. We also have to tell Ms. Fenster."

"Why do you have to do that?"

"You put Marcus and Milo in danger. You also endangered yourself. We have to report it."

I get a bad feeling. Ms. Fenster doesn't like me. I never should have touched that gun.

ONE HOUR LATER. I lie on top of my bed, looking at the ceiling.

I try not to think about what's going to happen next.

A car pulls up outside. I look out the window. Ms. Fenster gets out and walks to the front door.

She's going to take me away.

The door opens. I hear voices in the living room.

She's going to come in and tell me to pack my stuff.

There's a knock on my door. Ms. Fenster comes in with Mr. and Ms. Radley.

"Are you okay?" Ms. Fenster asks.

"It was an accident," I say. "I thought it was unloaded. I was going to give it to Mr. Radley."

"Why didn't you give it to the police when we were at your uncle's trailer?"

"I don't know. I wasn't thinking."

She looks in the closet and feels all my clothes. She does the same thing with the clothes in my dresser.

She lifts the mattress and pulls out the sock with the money in it. I hang my head and look at the floor.

"What are you doing with all this cash?" she asks.

"It was my uncle's. I was saving it for him."

"Not a good decision."

She goes outside my room with Mr. and Ms. Radley. I put my ear to the door.

"I have to think of Marcus and Milo," Ms. Fenster says. "It's dangerous to keep Roy here. You don't know what he's going to do. You can't trust him."

I try to keep listening. But their voices get lower, and I can't tell what they say.

I know she's going to take me.

But I hear her car leave.

Mr. and Ms. Radley come in and sit on the bed next to me.

"We talked about everything," Mr. Radley says. "She was going to take you out of here tonight. But there isn't a home where she can place you right now. You're going to stay with us until she can find one."

"But it was an accident. I was trying to do the right thing."

"You also had the fight," Mr. Radley says. "And you were shoplifting."

I look around the bedroom. I don't want to leave.

Why did I take the gun? Why did I pull the trigger?

13   HOLD ME

LATER. I lie in bed. The house is quiet.

I felt helpless when the gun went off.

It happened so fast.

I remember when Mom died. I'm so tired.

I close my eyes.

I'm ten years old. It's hot in the trailer. It's always hot, even at night.

I'm in my room. I try to sleep.

Mom and Jack move around in the kitchen.

One of them locks my door from the outside. They're cooking meth again.

I listen to the sounds from the kitchen. A pan falls on the floor.

"What's wrong with you?" Jack screams. "Can't you do anything right?"

Boom!

The trailer shakes. Smoke comes under the door.

Fire!

I jump out of bed. The smoke gets thicker. I can't breathe. I have to get out.

I pick up my chair and break the window. I climb outside. The glass cuts my feet.

Jack pulls me away from the

trailer. Flames shoot out the
kitchen windows.

Where's Mom?

Jack won't let go of me.

Where's Mom?

I sit in a jail cell. It's cold
and dark. The steel bars surround
me.

Mom sits next to me. She squeezes
my hand. "Roy, it's going to be
okay."

I look down. The skin on her hand
smokes. It's burned, like burned
meat.

I look into her eyes. She smiles.
The skin on her face cracks off.

No!

I feel arms around me. It's Ms.
Radley.

"It's going to be okay," she

says. "It's not real. You were
dreaming."

My face is wet. I've been crying.

It was a dream. But I can't get
it out of my head.

It feels good to have her hold
me.

14   TOUGH TIME

WEDNESDAY MORNING. ENGLISH. I'm
still tired from last night.

I put my head on my desk. I need
to close my eyes for a minute.

I like Marcus and Milo. It would
be nice to be their big brother.

Why did I take Uncle Frank's gun?
I should have left it in the
trailer.

I don't have anybody. I don't
want to leave the Radleys.

There's tapping on my shoulder. I
open my eyes and sit up. It's Henry.

Ms. Gulliver comes to the front of the classroom.

"The news article today is about the forest fires in Colorado," she says. "There were firefighters who lost their lives. Read it to yourself. You will then discuss it with your elbow partner."

She passes out the article.

I remember our trailer on fire. The flames blasted out the windows.

Mom was burning inside.

I look around the room. They don't know what it was like.

I can't take it. I have to get away.

I run out of the classroom.

OUTSIDE. I go to the food court and sit against the back wall where nobody will see me.

The tears start. I can't hold them back.

Ms. Fenster is going to take me away from the Radleys. She doesn't know what I'm going through. I'm trying to change.

The back door of the cafeteria opens. Dr. Vinson comes out with a cup of coffee in his hand.

I try to dry my face. But my sleeve is soaked.

"Roy, what's going on?" he asks.

"I got a hall pass from Ms. Gulliver. I just needed some fresh air."

I keep my eyes down. I don't want him to know I was crying.

"Can I see the pass?" he asks.

I reach into my pocket and give him an old hall pass from five days ago. He smiles when he looks at it.

"I guess we're a week behind," he says. "Come with me. Let's talk."

PRINCIPAL'S OFFICE. I sit across the desk from Dr. Vinson. I try to hide my face. I can't stop crying.

"How come you left Ms. Gulliver's class?" he asks.

I don't want to tell him. He won't understand.

"Everybody is gone now," I say. "My mom is dead. My uncle is in jail. And I will have to leave the Radleys."

"Who are the Radleys?"

"My foster parents. I accidentally shot a gun in their house."

"What were you doing with a gun?"

"It was my uncle's. I took it when the social worker came to get me. Everything I do goes bad. My grades. Fighting Donny. Sometimes I just can't take it."

The tears start again.

He passes me a box of tissues.

I look up. I see tears in his eyes.

"There are people at this school who care about you," Dr. Vinson says. "You don't have to go through this alone."

He picks up his phone and dials. "Mr. Radley?... This is Dr. Vinson from Edison High School... I have Roy in my office... Can you come over here?... He's having a tough time."

15 HAVE TO

THIRTY MINUTES LATER. I'm still in Dr. Vinson's office. Mr. Radley comes in.

I thought he would be mad about leaving work. But he smiles when he sees me.

"I found Roy by the cafeteria," Dr. Vinson says. "He seemed pretty upset about things. We talked for a long time."

"It's been tough at home," Mr. Radley says. "Is it okay if I check him out of school for about an hour?

I want to take him someplace where we can talk."

Dr. Vinson nods. "I think that will help."

BURGER HOUSE. It's almost empty when we get there. We order food and sit in the back.

"What happened?" Mr. Radley asks.

I try to hold back. But the tears come anyway.

Mr. Radley walks to the counter and comes back with some napkins so I can dry my face.

"I want to stay with you and Ms. Radley," I say. "I didn't mean to shoot the gun. I thought it was empty. I'm sorry about stealing the skateboard wheels. I promise not to fight again. And I won't lie anymore."

"Ms. Fenster was worried when she came over last night," Mr. Radley says. "It's not just about your own safety. It's also about Marcus and Milo."

I can't stop crying. I feel like a little kid. "I'm trying to do better. I'm begging you."

"There's something you need to know," Mr. Radley says. "I was a foster kid, too. I never knew my dad. My mom was on heroin. They took me from her when I was seven."

I can't believe he's saying this. I thought he was perfect.

"It was bad," he says. "I went from one foster home to another. Nobody wanted me."

"What happened?"

"I finally got put with some people who understood me. I had a foster dad who made me feel like his son."

I dry my eyes. I feel better.

"The question is this," Mr. Radley says. "What are you going to do? You can choose to do wrong and keep messing up. Or you can choose to do right."

I've never thought about choices. I've always thought bad things were just happening to me.

"You have to decide who you're going to be and make good decisions," Mr. Radley says. "You have to think about the consequences and choose to be responsible. If you do that, you will be okay."

I didn't think he would understand, but he does.

"I'm going to call Ms. Fenster after I take you back to school," he

says. "I will tell her everything
and see if I can change her mind.
But you have to make a decision. You
can't think like a kid anymore. You
have to think like an adult."

It's going to be hard. But I have
to do it.

16   WHAT IF?

THURSDAY MORNING. The twins come in and wake me. I try to smile and act happy for them. But it's hard.

If Ms. Fenster takes me today, this will be my last breakfast here. I hope Mr. Radley can change her mind.

I get dressed and go to the kitchen. Mr. Radley comes in and sits at the table with us.

"Any news from Ms. Fenster?" I ask.

"I called and left a message

again," he says. "Still nothing."

"Maybe that's a good sign," Ms. Radley says.

I hope she's right.

TIME FOR SCHOOL. I put on my helmet, grab my skateboard, and leave out the front door. Henry meets me at the corner.

"Roy, what's with the helmet?" he asks.

"I promised Ms. Radley I would wear it. I'm trying to stay with them."

"What do you mean?"

"I had a problem the other night. My social worker might move me to another family."

"What kind of a problem?"

"It's a long story. But I accidentally did something that was a bad idea."

"What happened yesterday when you ran out of Ms. Gulliver's class?"

"Things got to me when we were reading about the fire. It's a long story."

"Did you get in trouble?"

"Dr. Vinson found me and called Mr. Radley. He took me to Burger House, and we talked. I have to show that I'm responsible."

The light turns green. We skate another block and stop at the next red light.

"Donny was messing with somebody yesterday," Henry says.

"Who was it?"

"A new guy, somebody little. Donny pushed him in the hallway. Everybody was laughing."

"That's Donny. He always has to

bother somebody, especially if it's someone smaller than him."

"The guy was crying and mad at the same time," Henry says. "He had a look on his face like he wanted to kill Donny."

THE BELL RINGS. I leave history and go into the hall. Two girls walk in front of me.

"Did you hear about the new guy?" the first one asks. "I think his name is Gerald."

"What happened?" the second one asks.

"He brought a gun to school."

"How do you know?"

"He has it in his backpack. A girl in my math class told me."

I remember how I felt when I shot the gun in the Radley's house. It happened so fast.

I don't want to snitch. But what if he shoots somebody?

17   WISH I COULD

PASSING PERIOD. I reach the hallway outside my art class.

I should go in. But I keep walking.

I have to hurry.

I walk faster.

Then I run.

I'm breathing hard when I get to the main office.

Dr. Vinson comes in. "Roy, do you have a pass?"

"Can I talk to you?"

"Why don't you have a pass?"

"Please?"

I follow him into his office. I remember how I felt when the gun went off in my hand.

"Dr. Vinson, remember when you told us we could report things anonymously?"

"What's going on?"

"Some girls were talking. There's somebody at school with a gun."

He closes the door and pulls out his radio. "E-three to E-one."

"E-one, go."

"Possible four-seventeen on campus. Come to my office."

"Ten-four."

Two minutes pass. Officer Billups comes in the door. I give him the information. Two officers from the Conroy Police Department also come in.

Dr. Vinson gets on the PA system. "Attention. This is the principal. All staff, please begin lockdown procedures. All staff, begin lockdown procedures now."

Dr. Vinson turns to me. "Your name will not go out to anybody. Do not tell anyone about this except your parents."

I feel better now. I did the right thing.

LUNCH. I sit with Henry and Oscar at our table in the food court.

"Guess what," Oscar says. "That lockdown was about somebody with a gun."

"How do you know?" Henry asks.

"It was a guy named Gerald," Oscar says. "He's in my science class. The police came in and took him. People are saying he had a nine-millimeter in his backpack."

I eat my sandwich. I don't want them to know I told.

"And guess what else," Oscar says. "People are saying he was going to shoot Donny."

"What does Gerald look like?" Henry asks.

"He's a little guy," Oscar says. "Somebody quiet who looks like he would never hurt anybody."

I'm glad I told Dr. Vinson.

AFTER SCHOOL. Radley's house. I sit at the kitchen table with Marcus and Milo.

They're doing worksheets on the alphabet. They try so hard. It's fun to watch them work.

"Our teacher talked to us today

about doing the right thing," Milo says.

"Like what?" I ask.

"Like being safe. If you know something is wrong, and it could hurt someone, you have to tell somebody."

"Who do you tell?" I ask.

"You tell your teacher. But don't let the other kids hear you."

"That's a good idea," I say.

"Do you ever have problems at your school?" Marcus asks.

"Sometimes," I say. "That's why you have to report it. Do what your teacher tells you."

I feel like a big brother when I say that. I wish I could stay.

18   NEVER FORGET

LATE AFTERNOON. I lie on my bed and read over the essay I wrote for my health class. It's about making tough choices and trying to do the right thing.

I think about the guy who brought the gun to school. I wonder what's happening to him now.

The front door opens.

"I'm home," Mr. Radley calls out.

I hear his footsteps in the hall. He comes into my room.

"Roy, I heard what happened at

your school today," he says.

"Yeah. We had a lockdown."

"Do you know the reason?"

"The principal sent a letter home. A guy brought a gun to school. They arrested him."

"I found out more this afternoon," Mr. Radley says. "A student heard about the gun and made an anonymous report to the principal. The guy with the gun was getting ready to shoot another student. Then he was going to shoot himself. He wrote a suicide note."

I look at the floor where the bullet went through.

"It could have been bad," Mr. Radley says. "The student who reported it is a hero."

I want to tell him what I did. But I can't.

EVENING. The twins are in bed now. I sit at the kitchen table doing math. It seems like it's starting to get easier.

Mr. Radley's phone rings. I wonder if it's Ms. Fenster. I get a bad feeling.

"Thanks for telling me," Mr. Radley says. "I know it's hard for you when something like this happens... I'll tell him right now. Thanks for calling."

I'm sure it's bad news. I'm surprised when he smiles.

"How come you didn't tell us?" he asks.

"Tell what?"

"That was Dr. Vinson. He said you told him about the gun. You probably saved two lives today."

Ms. Radley hugs me.

"I didn't know what to do at first. I didn't want to be a snitch."

"You made an adult decision," Mr. Radley says. "You did the right thing."

He looks me in the eye and shakes my hand like I'm a man.

I wish I could stay here. I wish he could be my dad.

But it's all going to end soon.

ONE HOUR LATER. My homework is done. I put everything into my backpack.

Mr. and Ms. Radley come into the kitchen and sit across from me.

"What made you decide to report the guy with the gun?" Mr. Radley asks.

"I didn't want anybody to get hurt. And I thought about what you told me."

"What was that?"

"You said to think about the consequences. I thought about what would happen if he pulled the trigger."

The Radleys have been good to me. I will never forget them.

19 FAMILY NOW

FRIDAY MORNING. Henry and I skate to school.

It's my second day of wearing a helmet. I told Ms. Radley I would.

We stop at the red light on Neptune Street.

"Roy, what's wrong?" Henry asks.

"The Radleys want me to stay. But it's the social worker. She's the one who says I have to leave. It's only a matter of time before she takes me."

We cross the street and skate.

This could be my last day at Edison High School.

HISTORY. We're having a review today. Mr. Rubio hands out the study guides.

The door opens. It's a blue slip for me to see Dr. Vinson.

I wonder what it's about.

PRINCIPAL'S OFFICE. Dr. Vinson smiles and waves me in.

"I want to commend you for what you did yesterday," he says. "You're getting the Edison Merit Award."

He puts a medal around my neck. It feels heavy, like it's the real thing. He gives me a certificate and shakes my hand.

I read the words: *This Certificate of Merit is hereby*

awarded to Roy Perkins. Thank you
for your courage, sound judgment,
and service to Edison High School.

I look at my name again. It's
really me.

"I remember the day when I gave
you detention for throwing the book
out the window," Dr. Vinson says.
"You're a different person now."

"What do you mean?"

"It was all over the school that
Gerald had a gun," he says. "Out of
all the students who knew, you were
the only one who reported it. You
showed a lot by what you did."

"I just didn't want anybody to
get hurt."

"That's what I mean," he says. "I
also looked at your grades on School
View. You're doing all your homework
now. And your grades are coming up."

I was mad at everything when I threw the book. I don't feel that way now.

"You're turning things around," Dr. Vinson says. "And it's happening because of the decisions you're making. I'm proud of you."

After all the bad things I've done, I never thought he would be proud of me.

SCHOOL'S OUT. I skate home with Henry.

If Ms. Fenster takes me from the Radleys this evening, this could be the last time I skate with him.

RADLEY'S HOUSE. The twins sit at the kitchen table, doing their homework. I sit across from them and open my backpack.

"How was school today?" I ask.

"We're learning a song about the Pilgrims," Marcus says. "It's for the music show."

"When is that?"

"It's on the Tuesday before Thanksgiving," Milo says. "You're coming."

They don't know I'm leaving. How will I tell them?

EIGHT O'CLOCK. I'm still doing my math homework.

Mr. Radley's phone rings.

"Hi, Ms. Fenster," he says. "Thanks for calling... I also tried calling you this morning... Did you get my email?... I'm sure it's been tough... Roy has really been trying... Is that the final decision?... Thank you."

He ends the call. I get ready for the bad news.

But he smiles.

"You're staying," he says. "And she's recommending that you remain here on a permanent placement."

He hugs me. Ms. Radley and the twins run in. She kisses me on the cheek and wraps her arms around me. The twins hug me too.

I have a family now.

20 HOME

TWO WEEKS LATER. ENGLISH. I take my seat and get ready for class to start.

We're having a test today. I stayed up late studying last night. I'm tired, but I'm ready.

Ms. Gulliver comes to the front of the classroom. She looks at each of us.

"I was thinking about all of you last night when I was checking papers," she says. "Many of you have been working hard. And I've seen great improvement."

"Remember this," she says. "You can be as successful as you decide to be. Many of you have chosen to work hard in this class. That's why your grades are coming up."

I remember how it was three months ago. I didn't care about school. And I wasn't trying.

It's different now. I'm not perfect. But I feel good about myself.

I have a future.

AFTER SCHOOL. Henry and I skate down Neptune Street. We stop at the corner for a red light.

"Roy, do you want to skate tomorrow?" he asks.

"Can't do it," I say. "Mr. Radley is taking me to see Uncle Frank.

They sent him to Joplin State Prison."

"I thought you never wanted to see your uncle again."

"I don't feel that way anymore. He wrote me a letter. He's sorry for what he did."

"What about Sunday?" Henry asks. "Do you want to skate then?"

"Can't do that, either. We're going to see my mom's grave in Raymond. All of us are going, Mr. and Ms. Radley, the twins, and me."

The light turns green. I skate one more block and turn right onto Orchard Avenue.

I stop at the yellow house with the big tree and flowers.

I remember the night when I first came here.

I felt like I was being thrown

away. But the Radleys took me in.
And they want to adopt me.

I climb the steps and open the
front door.

I'm home.

ACKNOWLEDGMENTS

I would like to express my sincere gratitude to everyone who gave me feedback while I was writing this book.

COFFEE HOUSE WRITERS GROUP: Nicholas Chiazza, Robyn Dolan, Synida Fontes, Samantha Hancox-Li, Helene Hoffmann, J. Bryan Jones, Alex Khansa, John Lowell, Dollie Mason, Scott McClelland, Dav Pauli, Jean Pliska, Emily Wiley, AnneLise Wilhelmsen, and Dennis Wolverton.

NOVEL INTENSIVE COURSE FOR WRITERS: Ara Grigorian and Janis Thomas.

SOCIETY OF CHILDREN'S BOOK WRITERS AND ILLUSTRATORS: Tim Burke, Debra

Garfinkle, Emily Heebner, Bryan Hilson, Jessica Parra, Beverly Plas, Linda Ruddy, Erika Turner, Jesper Widen, Sonja Wilbert, and AnneLise Wilhelmson.

SOUTHERN CALIFORNIA WRITERS CONFERENCE: Jennifer Silva Redmond, Dr. Uwe Stender, Jennifer Chen Tran, and Claudia Whitsitt.

Thank you, Pam Sheppard, for your advice on creating this series.

Thank you, Laura Perkins, for your careful editing and thoughtful guidance.

Thank you, Betty-Jean, for your patience, your suggestions, your love, and for being my wife.

ABOUT THE AUTHOR

 My dream of becoming a writer started at Whitworth University. I was lucky to have a teacher, Dr. Tammy Reid, who believed in me and encouraged me. After college, I began a career as an educator, teaching reading and English at a middle school in Los Angeles. I later served as a high-school principal. During my many years of working with young people, I observed that every student can succeed. You can be successful if you set high goals, work hard every day, and never give up. Believe in yourself and strive to achieve your dreams.

ADDITIONAL TITLES

TAKEN AWAY. Miles Pruitt has been struggling in high school. When his dad is sent to prison, things get worse. How will he pick himself up and move forward?

NO PLACE TO HIDE. Ninth grader Owen Daniels has struggled with reading since first grade. A caring teacher helps him, he becomes a strong reader, and his grades improve. But he must learn to believe in himself.

ALL ALONE. Tenth grader Elgin Hobbs seems fine on the outside. But he's failing classes, his divorced parents fight, and his mom is an alcoholic. How can he rise above these troubles and keep going?

Lightning Source UK Ltd.
Milton Keynes UK
UKHW010631100621
385271UK00001B/184